GREAT SCARRIER REEF

MONSTER HIGH™

Welcome to the
Great Scarrier Reef

Adapted by
Margaret Green

Based on the screenplay by

Nina Bargiel and
Shane Amsterdam

LITTLE, BROWN & COMPANY
LB kids

Little, Brown and Company

Hachette Book Group
1290 Avenue of the Americas, New York, NY 10104
Visit us at lb-kids.com

LB kids is an imprint of Little, Brown and Company.
The LB kids name and logo are trademarks of Hachette Book Group, Inc.

The publisher is not responsible for websites (or their content)
that are not owned by the publisher.

First Edition: April 2016

ISBN 978-0-316-30127-5

10 9 8 7 6 5 4 3 2 1

CW

Printed in the United States of America

It was almost summer, and the ghouls were having the time of their lives. Clawdeen Wolf, Frankie Stein, and Draculaura were excited for their upcoming dance recital, but they were having trouble following Toralei's crazy choreography.

"Hey, ghouls! Looking...great?" Lagoona Blue tried to sound convincing as she entered the Vampitheater in the middle of rehearsals.

"Come join us!" said Frankie.

"Oh, I couldn't possibly," replied Lagoona. "**I'm a swimmer**, not a dancer."

"Well, if you want to make yourself useful, I need someone to organize the wrap party," Toralei told Lagoona.

Lagoona agreed. But as the other girls left, she stayed behind and went onstage. When she was sure she was alone, she turned the music back on and started dancing—she was **fintastic**!

Lagoona didn't know that her boyfriend, Gil, was watching her. When he started clapping, she froze.

She made Gil promise not to tell anyone about her stage fright, but Toralei overheard Lagoona's secret.

The next night at the recital, when Toralei's routine was not as purrfect as she'd hoped, she pulled up the curtain so the audience could see Lagoona dancing backstage. Sure enough, Lagoona froze again. As she tried to run off the stage, her foot got caught in one of the ropes raising the curtain—sending her belly-up in front of the whole school.

The embarrassment didn't stop there. Someone videotaped the incident and uploaded the video online, where it quickly went viral! Lagoona was furious with Toralei. She decided to disinvite her from her own wrap party.

When Toralei finally found the ghouls partying near the Monster High pool, she headed straight for Lagoona.

"Prepare to be filleted!" she shrieked, grabbing a creepcake and lunging at Lagoona.

No one noticed that the water in the pool had begun to bubble and swirl. Lagoona dodged Toralei's incoming creepcake, and Toralei tumbled right into the churning water. Lagoona jumped in to save her—and was quickly **swept into the current!** Gil, Clawdeen, Draculaura, and Frankie formed a monster chain to pull them out, but the vortex was too strong. One by one, they were sucked down into the pool!

When the vortex finally stopped spinning, the friends found themselves deep below the ocean.

"Where are we?" Frankie asked.

"More like...*what* are we?" Draculaura replied. They had all been fishified!

"I'm getting hydrophobic," Toralei complained. "Lagoona, change me back right *meow*!"

An unfamiliar voice broke in. "Oh, Lagoona didn't do that. I did."
It was Posea Reef, the daughter of Poseidon, Guardian of the
Sea. She explained that she'd brought them to her kingdom so
Lagoona could move past what had been troubling her.

"Face **your deepest fear** and find your way home,"
Posea advised.

"Um, I do that...how?" asked Lagoona. But Posea had disappeared. The ghouls and Gil followed her Sea-Mares even deeper into the ocean, where they came across an underwater Vampitheater filled with dancing, shimmering lights.

"Why does this look so familiar?" Lagoona wondered.

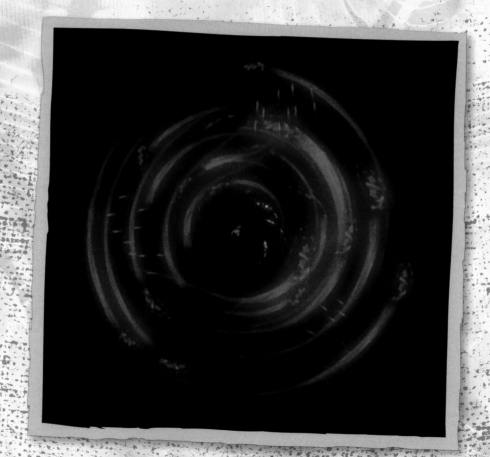

As Lagoona and her friends swam closer, they realized the dancing lights were actually sea creatures performing an intricate routine. Lagoona recognized the star performer as her childhood friend, Kala Mer'ri. She remembered the last time she danced with Kala....

"Even the big ol' Kraken could do this step," she had told Kala, trying to be encouraging. But Kala got angry and tied Lagoona's shoes together. The audience had laughed at her, and she hadn't been able to overcome her stage fright since.

Lagoona, Gil, and the other ghouls left the Vampitheater and went to visit Lagoona's family. Her dad made Vegemite sandwiches and told them to watch out for the Kraken, a huge, dangerous underwater creature.

As they brainstormed how to get home, Kala appeared in front of them.

"I wanted to see if you ghouls have the guts to compete in the Siren of the Sea talent show tomorrow night," she said. "Are you afraid to take me on, Lagoona?"

"I'll do it," Lagoona said shakily. **"I'll dance."**

That night, Kala's
friend Peri Serpentine,
daughter of the Hydra,
appeared at Lagoona's
window. Her twin sister,
Pearl, appeared as well,
but she was pretending to be
asleep. "Kala is so fearless because she goes down to the Deepest
Dark and looks the Kraken dead in the eye," Peri told Lagoona.

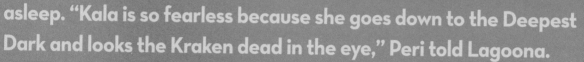

As soon as Peri swam away from Lagoona's
house, her twin, Pearl, "woke up" and grinned. Kala
was waiting for them around the corner.

Peri quickly realized
what had happened:
Pearl and Kala had
tricked her into telling
Lagoona she needed to
face the Kraken!

And Lagoona had fallen for it, hook, line, and sinker. She was now convinced that to become fearless, she needed to look the Kraken in the eye. When she told her ghoulfriends what her plan was, they begged her not to go.

But when Lagoona insisted it was what she needed to do, her ghoulfriends said they would join her. They weren't about to let Lagoona face a giant sea monster alone!

Lagoona and her ghoulfriends made the long journey down
to the Kraken's lair—but he was *not* happy to see them!

The ghouls swam away as fast as they could, using their new
fintastic abilities to fight off the angry Kraken. When they made
it back to the surface, Lagoona couldn't believe she'd done it!

"Now are you ready to take on Kala at the Siren of the Sea?"
Clawdeen asked.

"There's only one way to find out!" replied Lagoona.

Under the stage before the talent show, Kala revealed to Lagoona that looking the Kraken in the eye wouldn't really make her fearless. Lagoona's newfound confidence went down the drain.

"So what if there's no magic?" Frankie told her. "You were brave enough to face a Kraken! What's a little dance show after that?"

But when it came time for Lagoona's solo, the crowd's attention made her freeze. Everyone started to laugh.

"Hey, stop it!" Gil shouted at the hecklers. "I've seen this ghoul dance—and she's fintastic."

"Even though she was scared, she swam out onstage and tried," Frankie chimed in.

"So maybe you should try clapping instead of laughing!" Toralei added.

The Monster High gang tried to make their way out of the Vampitheater as Kala took the stage, but the crowd started chanting Lagoona's name. Enraged, Kala made a sound none of the ghouls had heard before.

Out of the depths of the dark waters rose the Kraken! Lagoona, Gil, and the others led the giant squid away from Great Scarrier Reef and toward Posea's garden, where they persuaded the undersea goddess to send them back to Monster High.

The ghouls and Gil arrived safely at their school, back on two legs instead of fins. They didn't have long to celebrate, however. A geyser shot out of the pool, and on top of it was Kala—riding the Kraken!

"Great Kraken, destroy it all!" Kala commanded. She pointed at Lagoona. "Starting with her!"

"SWIM—I mean, **RUN**!" cried Lagoona. The ghouls scattered as the Kraken crashed and ripped through Monster High. They met in the Vampitheater to come up with a plan.

"It's like Kala controls the Kraken," Frankie noted.

"That's why I need you to distract him," Lagoona said. "The only chance we have of saving Monster High is for me to persuade Kala to call him off."

Toralei's wild dance moves finally came in handy—she distracted the Kraken while Lagoona begged Kala to help.

Kala refused. She called the Kraken to her, and he quickly captured Lagoona in his tentacles.

"Why are you doing this?" Lagoona asked.

"You'll never understand what it's like for someone to hate you for what you are!" said Kala.

"But no one is an outcast at Monster High," Lagoona explained. "So take me if you have to. But leave Monster High alone."

"So at Monster High I wouldn't be judged for being different?" Kala asked uncertainly.

"Never!" Lagoona reassured her.

Kala looked at the Kraken. "Put her down, Dad."

"Dad?!?!" Lagoona squeaked.

"DAD?!?!" her ghoulfriends echoed.

As the Kraken helped repair Monster High, Lagoona apologized to her old friend. "I'm so sorry I thought your dad was evil, just because of his looks."

"I'm sorry I made fun of you for going belly-up," Kala said.

"It's all in the past, and the past is what made me and you what we are today." Lagoona pulled Kala into a big hug.

The next day, Lagoona threw a **pool party** to celebrate the rebuilding of Monster High.

"Am I invited to *this* party?" Toralei asked Lagoona.

"Of course. Every monster is!" she replied. Even Kala, Peri, and Pearl showed up!

Lagoona beamed proudly as she watched her friends—old and new—using the Kraken's tentacles as waterslides. Not only had she faced her deepest fear—she'd **made friends with it!**